CW00858790

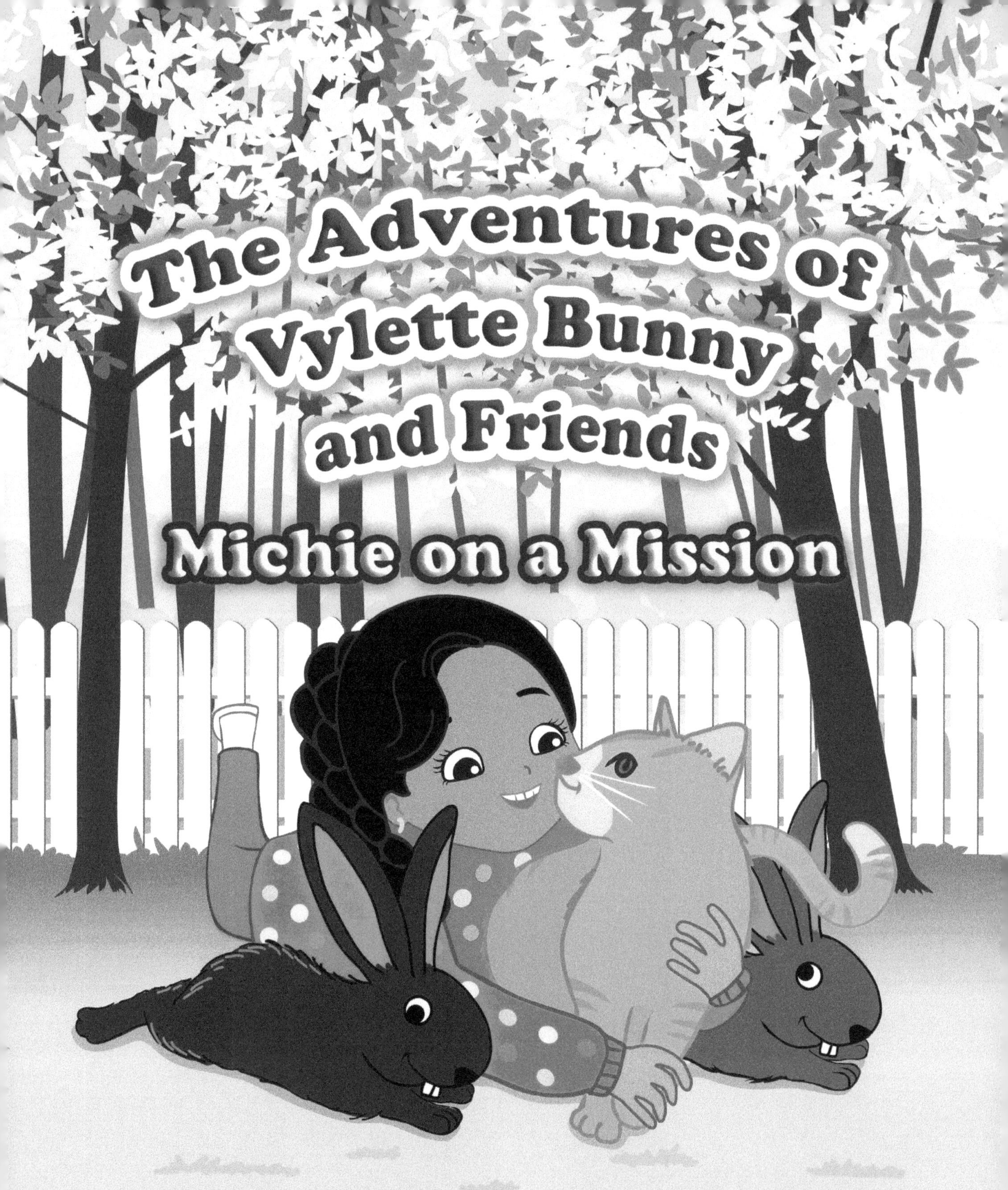

By Michelle Crichton Illustrated by i Cenizal

The Adventures of Vylette Bunny and Friends

Tellwell Talent
www.tellwell.ca

ISBN
978-0-2288-7314-3 (Hardcover)
978-0-2288-7312-9 (Paperback)
978-0-2288-7313-6 (eBook)

Dedication:

I dedicate this book to my family and friends, especially Uncle Henry for truly believing in the characters. Thank you all so much for supporting *The Adventures of Vylette Bunny and Michie*. Because of your enthusiasm, I was able to create another story with important messages. To iCenizal (Illustrator) for bringing my visions to life on each page. To Jen (Editor) and Sem (Production Manager at Tellwell). To my dear pet Bugs, you will never be forgotten. To Tuffy, your strength and independence during hardship is an inspiration for many!

Tuffy was a solid orange tabby with a bright mind and an independent spirit. He was friendly and he liked people, but he truly loved to be on his own. Lately, he enjoyed roaming around neighbourhoods. He thought, "Nobody needs to worry about me. I can survive anything!"

Vylette Bunny had been living with Michie and her family for a while now, and she had learned the house rules. She even had a special room for chewing toys and eating when nobody was home. The pet shop that Vylette and her brother Chocolat lived in before had now become a shelter for animals in need of a proper home. Ms. Berkley, who ran the pet shop, now ran the centre. Since Michie had learned how to properly care for a bunny, her family allowed her to take in Vylette's brother, Chocolat, from the Adoption Centre. Chocolat and Vylette were excited to be reunited.

SMARTY PANTS
ANIMALS

The bunnies enjoyed their play time with Michie, and when *Smarty Pants Animals* was on the television, binkies were performed by the bunnies! “So nice to see the bunnies getting along so well. They’re very well-behaved!” remarked Michie’s mom.

One day, Michie noticed a large orange cat taking a stroll in her neighbourhood. “You’re adorable! Where did you come from, kitty?” said Michie.

Tuffy looked at Michie with large sparkling emerald eyes and said, “MEOW!”

Michie gave Tuffy a gentle pat on the head, and he walked away while waving his tail to form the letter “S.” Michie wondered “Does he have a home?”

As she entered the house, she told her parents about the cat.

“Mom, Dad! Guess what! When I was coming home, I bumped into a nice cat. I’ve never seen him before, but he let me pat him. I wonder if I’ll see him again. I hope that he’s okay.” Michie felt concerned.

“He probably has a home. I wouldn’t worry,” responded Michie’s mom.

Vylette and Chocolat were listening.

“You hear that? Michie sounds very delighted with this nice cat. Will she eventually forget about us?” wondered Chocolat.

“Everybody knows how Michie loves animals, but whatever you do, please don’t start chewing anything. Trust me: the humans in this family might try to get rid of us!” replied Vylette.

“Let’s not make any mischief!” said Chocolat.

The bunnies remembered that they once lived within Ms. Berkley’s care until they were brought home by Michie. If Tuffy became the new pet, would the bunnies be separated? Where would they live?

A few days later, Michie took the bunnies outside to hop around while wearing their leashes. Guess who appeared? Tuffy came up to Michie, looking for another pat on the head.

“Look who it is!” exclaimed Michie.

Tuffy thought, “The girl seems nice, but who are the bunnies? There’s only one furball that runs this neighbourhood: ME!” Tuffy liked the feeling of being around Michie because she did not seem like a threat. He could sense that she was a true animal lover.

Vylette said to Chocolat, “Look at Michie. She’s not even paying any attention to us! She has a new friend now.”

“What’s so special about him?” said Chocolat.

The two bunnies felt jealous. Tuffy felt threatened about his position in the community!

When Tuffy followed Michie home, she spoke with a neighbour about the cat.

“I’ve seen him around. He comes and goes, and we leave food out for him. No idea where he came from,” said Sally the neighbour. “We call him Tuffy since he was walking in the cold the other night. He seems quite tough and brave.”

“Wow, does he need help? What if he’s somebody’s lost pet? I can’t imagine what I’d do if I lost my bunnies,” said Michie. As the bunnies listened, they felt happy to know that Michie would not want anything unfortunate to happen to them.

“He arrives at different times of the day and runs off after eating, so capturing him has been hard. He sleeps in a building garage,” expressed Sally.

“This isn’t good,” thought Michie. “Winter is just around the corner, and he can’t be outside like this,” said Michie to Sally. Meanwhile, Tuffy looked at Vylette and Chocolat. The bunnies opened their mouths and flashed their front teeth to show that they were capable of biting. Tuffy opened his mouth and displayed his teeth as well. The animals were now in competition, and it was team Vylette and Chocolat against lonely Tuffy.

“Mom, Dad! Look who followed me home! Tuffy, the cat I told you about. Can we take him in until we can find him a proper home?” Michie knew that Tuffy’s stay would be temporary because there might not be enough space with all three animals.

“I don’t know if this will work. Where will Tuffy stay? Cats are carnivores. Tuffy might hunt rabbits,” said Michie’s mom.

“The giant cage for the bunnies isn’t being used anymore, so Tuffy can use it. Also, the bunnies have their own space in the house, so we can keep Tuffy away when necessary!” As the ideas came to Michie’s mind, she felt thrilled!

“The nearby Value Shop has inexpensive pet supplies, like litter boxes, litter, and cat food,” said Michie’s dad.

"You see! Where there's a will, there's always a way, eh Mom? You always say that!" said Michie enthusiastically with a wink.

"Well, yes, I did say that before, but this is different," responded Michie's mom.

"Please, Mom! I promise to do my best to find out where Tuffy belongs."

"As long as your dad is okay with this situation. Ahem!... And are you okay with this?" said Michie's mom, looking at Michie's dad.

"Yes. The cat needs our help."

Michie ran to the Value Shop and used some of her birthday savings to obtain the essentials for Tuffy. Meanwhile, Michie's parents brought Tuffy inside. They left Vylette and Chocolat in their special room for now.

After picking up the items, Michie stopped by Ms. Berkley's centre.

"So, you've found a homeless cat? That's awfully kind of you and your family to welcome him inside," said Ms. Berkley.

"Do you have any room for him here?" asked Michie.

"I'm just like you, and I love animals a lot, but I'm at my maximum capacity. Animals need enough space to stay healthy and happy. I might have more room in six weeks," replied Ms. Berkley. "You could put up posters in the area to see if the cat is lost. You can continue to feed him, but please be careful. If he's an abandoned cat, he might be aggressive. Does the cat look like he's in any distress?"

"No, he seems fine, but he doesn't have a collar," responded Michie.

"If you bring him here, I can check to see if he has a microchip. This will tell us if he has an owner," said Ms. Berkley.

Adoption Centre

“That sounds amazing! This could solve Tuffy’s mystery!” said Michie.

Michie felt hopeful. With a bit of help and a strong will, she was bent on finding the answer to Tuffy’s problem! She would now begin “Operation Help Tuffy.”

Michie put out the litter box and the food for Tuffy. He seemed quite comfortable in the house! Michie even gave him a cat toy to keep him entertained. He knew how to use the litter box, which seemed unusual for a stray.

Meanwhile, Vylette and Chocolat noticed what was going on.

“He’s taking over our Michie’s attention!” said Vylette.

“Right! Soon there won’t be any Michie for us. We’ve got to think of a mischievous plan to get rid of this Tuffy!” said Chocolat.

“Very true!” said Vylette. The bunnies put their heads together and wiggled their noses in agreement. They brainstormed troublesome ideas!

The next day, Michie and her dad brought Tuffy to the Adoption Centre. After using the scanning device, Ms. Berkley said, “Unfortunately, Tuffy doesn’t have a microchip. Therefore, we don’t know where he belongs.”

“Okay, I’ll keep you posted. Thanks again, Ms. Berkley,” said Michie.

Since Michie enjoyed being creative, she designed a found cat poster and had it photocopied. She placed the posters on poles, on a notice board at the local grocery store, at her school, and anywhere else she could think of! It was a lot of work, but Michie knew that she could not give up. She felt anxious to find Tuffy a home but knew that this could take time.

FOUND
CAT

Days later, Vylette and Chocolat were chatting about their plan for "Operation Remove Tuffy." Their goal was to discourage Tuffy from wanting to stay.

"So, you'll use your teeth to turn over Tuffy's food bowl, right little sister?" said Chocolat.

"That used to be my silver bowl. My front teeth are still strong. I can handle it! Nobody touches my bowl!" said Vylette.

"Yes, and he took our cage too. What a thief!" replied Chocolat.

The bunnies did not want their belongings to be given to Tuffy. They felt that it was unfair. Unfortunately, Michie had no way of knowing what the bunnies were thinking, but she had noticed them huddling together more since Tuffy had arrived.

While Tuffy was sleeping, Vylette went to the silver bowl of cat food and turned it over. The food was now lying on the kitchen floor. Vylette quickly hopped away.

“Good job!” said Chocolat to Vylette.

Shortly after, Tuffy woke up and went to the bowl. “How strange. Michie doesn’t usually leave food on the ground for me,” he thought.

“HAHA!” laughed Vylette and Chocolat. When Tuffy turned around, he saw the two bunnies at a distance. Tuffy noticed the prankish looks on their faces.

“I just know that they did this,” thought Tuffy. “In this world, you can only really count on yourself,” he said to himself.

Tuffy felt that being in Michie’s home was holding him back from being independent. Outside, he would not be concerned about the bunnies causing him trouble. He could find his meals without any problems.

Michie came into the kitchen and saw Tuffy’s spilled food.

“Tuffy! Did you accidentally knock your food over? What a mess! Let me get some new food for you,” said Michie. She cleaned up the heap and gave him more food. Since Tuffy had a hunch that he was unwelcome, he ate while keeping one eye on the bunnies.

“New idea!” said Vylette to Chocolat. “How about I chew on Mom’s favourite wooden chair in the living room and make it look like Tuffy scratched it?” The bunnies had noticed Tuffy’s habit of lightly sharpening his claws on furniture.

“Yes, sister! This is a wonderful idea,” said Chocolat.

Off Vylette went to chomp a few bites into the legs of the chair. The bites looked like scrapes from a cat’s nail.

When Michie’s mom came home, she saw the damage.

“TUFFY! My wooden chair! This is too much. We need to find you a home soon!” blurted Michie’s mom.

Michie came in with Tuffy and they saw the scrapes. "Mom, Tuffy has been well-behaved so far. He didn't do this. Maybe those are older marks from when Vylette used to chew everything."

"No, this is new. I'm very disappointed that we're going through this all over again," said Michie's mom.

Michie looked at Tuffy and could not help feeling sorry for him. She was not sure where the marks came from, but she was confident that Tuffy was not the cause. Her intentions to help Tuffy were good, but was this becoming a problem for the family?

"I've sharpened my claws a little but nothing like that. Those bunnies are trying to get me into trouble," thought Tuffy.

The next day, Chocolat and Vylette had another meeting.

"I've got the absolute prank for Tuffy!" said Chocolat.

"What is it?" asked Vylette.

"Remember the episode of *Smarty Pants Animals* when a cucumber was placed behind a cat? The cat jumped in the air because it thought that the cucumber was a snake. Michie left us a small cucumber for nibbling. I could roll the cucumber over to Tuffy's tail when he least expects it. Hilarious!" said Chocolat.

"Sounds good to me!" said Vylette.

While Tuffy was drinking water from the silver bowl and his back was turned, brave Chocolat rolled the cucumber over. He had to be quiet and work very quickly. As the cucumber touched Tuffy's tail, Chocolat leaped away. Tuffy jumped into the air, thinking that a snake was behind him. When he looked again, he realized that it was not a snake but another sudden joke. Tuffy was tiring from the pranks, and he did not trust the bunnies. The bunnies did not trust Tuffy either.

When Michie came around, Tuffy began meowing. He desperately wanted to exit the house. He waited near the front door.

“No, Tuffy. It’s not smart for me to let you go free again. I’m finding you a decent home, remember?”

As Michie’s brother opened the door and came in, Tuffy decided to quickly run outside!

“TUFFY, NO!” cried Michie in frustration.

Tuffy walked quickly throughout the neighbourhood and Michie followed him, trying to lure him back. Michie felt like “Operation Help Tuffy” was going down the drain fast. She felt very saddened because she had hoped to see the best outcome for Tuffy.

The sun had set, which made it difficult to see outside. Michie kept walking around and calling “Tuffy!” but she lost him, and so she went back home.

“You did your best with Tuffy. Wild animals like that don’t want to be controlled. Look at what happened to the chair!” said Michie’s mom.

“I don’t believe that Tuffy did that. If he had, how come other objects in the house don’t have big scratches?” replied Michie.

She needed to be alone to process what had happened and to calm herself down. She dearly loved and missed Tuffy. She went to her room and pulled out her sketch book. She began drawing a picture of Tuffy, and then she worked on a poem about him.

Afterwards, she went to play with Vylette and Chocolat.

“I didn’t want him to escape. There could be danger out there and the streets aren’t safe,” Michie said softly, confiding her feelings to the bunnies.

They wiggled their noses against hers. Vylette gave Michie a “koosh.”

“You know something, Chocolat?” said Vylette. “Just because Michie is helping somebody else, that doesn’t mean she loves us any less.”

“You’re right. We’re lucky because we have a loving caregiver and home. Tuffy doesn’t. I regret our mischief. Everybody needs a bit of help sometimes, and right now Tuffy needs it the most. We wanted him to leave, but now that he's gone, our Michie is upset. This isn't good. We only wanted her for ourselves," said Chocolat with a heavy heart.

The bunnies were unhappy because Michie was unhappy. Michie's wish to help Tuffy find a home did not seem possible.

For the next week, Michie tried to take her mind away from worrying about Tuffy. Michie enjoyed spending time with her family and the bunnies, but Vylette and Chocolat felt her sadness about Tuffy.

"I wish that there was something we could do to fix this," said Vylette.

"I know, but we can't do anything as we're not allowed to leave the house unless we're supervised," responded Chocolat.

A few days passed and the phone suddenly rang. Michie answered the call.

"Hello, I'm looking for my lost cat and I saw your ad," said a strange voice.

"Sorry, but the cat ran away. I haven't seen him since," she replied.

At that moment, guess who appeared near the house? It was Tuffy, but Michie's eyes were looking away from the window.

Vylette and Chocolat spotted Tuffy through the window! "There he is! It sounds like Michie is speaking with another human about Tuffy. We need to get her attention immediately!" said Vylette.

"AHA! I'll use my teeth to pick away at her pants," said Chocolat.

Chocolat hopped towards Michie's leg and gave a forceful yet playful bite near the bottom of Michie's pants.

"Chocolat, what's the matter? I'm on the phone. I'll play with you afterwards," said Michie. Chocolat nipped again but Michie ignored him.

"Oh, this isn't working. I'd better hop in and bite too!" said Vylette.

Vylette galloped over and nipped away at the other leg.

“What’s going on?” blurted out Michie. She looked around and then out the window. Chocolat and Vylette stopped chewing. “Hello, the cat IS OUTSIDE! I’m going to run and grab him. Please hold!” said Michie to the caller. “TUFFY! Welcome back!” said Michie.

Without a fight, Tuffy allowed Michie to lift him inside the house and place him in the cage.

“I’ve now captured him, but how do I know that you’re really the owner?” inquired Michie.

“Can you please meet me with the cat at Ms. Berkley’s Centre in an hour? I’ll prove it!” said the mysterious voice.

“Alright, I’ll be there,” Michie agreed hopefully.

Michie ran into the kitchen. “Mom, Dad! I caught Tuffy again, and his owner just called. They want me to meet them at Ms. Berkley’s in an hour!”

“Just to be safe, I’ll go with you to meet this person. How about that?” said Michie’s mom.

“Sounds like a plan!” said Michie. They put Tuffy in a pet carrier and got ready to go. While he was waiting in the carrier, the bunnies bounced over to have a quick chat.

“We’re sorry for all those pranks and for chasing you away. We were worried that you’d take over Michie and our home. We were worried that we’d get separated. Now we know that’s not true. Can we be friends?” said Vylette.

“Apology accepted and friends we are! Michie will always do the right thing. She’ll never let you go. Your pranks were clever but know that I’m the master at tricks!” said Tuffy with a grin.

When Michie arrived at the centre, Ms. Berkley and a tall lady with ebony-coloured hair, a dark blue coat, and fashionable eyeglasses were waiting inside.

“You must be Michie. I’m Joan, Kurry’s owner. Pleased to meet you!”

“Hi, Joan. Kurry? We call him Tuffy since he’s very independent and tough.”

“Yes, that sounds like my cat!” laughed Joan gently. “Let me have a closer look at him.”

Michie opened the carrier and Joan observed the patterns in Kurry’s fur. She stared into his face and spoke to him. He responded by reaching out with his paw and saying “PURRRR!” He formed an “S” with his tail again.

“Yes, that’s him, alright,” said Joan. “When I blow my whistle, Kurry will do a trick. Would you like to see?”

Centre

“Absolutely!” responded Michie. They removed him from the pet carrier to see what would happen next. As the harmonic sound of the bright red whistle blew, Kurry did a circular jig on the ground and then finished with a playful “GRRRR!”

“WOW!” said Michie with wide eyes.

“This is one of his tricks. Thank you so much for reuniting us. I was very worried about you, Kurry. The day he ran away, the mail carrier was knocking, and just as I opened the door, he bolted outside. I was planning on bringing him to a clinic to get him microchipped and to place a collar around his neck. He was a rescue cat who became my pet. Sometimes he likes to be outdoors, and I make sure that he’s supervised. I’ll definitely see that he gets microchipped,” promised Joan.

“I’m happy that I was able to help Kurry. Thanks to my pet bunnies for nipping my attention today, I was able to get him back inside the house,” said Michie.

“What a happy ending!” said Ms. Berkeley.

Tuffy thought, “I enjoyed my freedom, but I’m glad to see Joan again. I understand why those bunnies were trying to keep Michie to themselves. She’s an outstanding caregiver.”

Centre

Back at home, Michie immediately checked on Vylette and Chocolat.

“I’m thankful that my parents allowed me to help Kurry find his owner. I’m also thankful to you both for your help. No matter what, you two will always be my favourite bunnies in the world. Always remember that Michie loves you,” said Michie.

Chocolat and Vylette looked at each other and then they watched Michie. They rubbed their heads together and Michie wiggled her nose against each of theirs.

“We helped Tuffy and Michie. We did good!” said Vylette to her brother.

As Michie walked away with an enormous smile, she gave herself a pat on the back. She said softly, “Well done, Michie. With a bit of hard work, determination, and some help from a few people, you saved the day.”

CHOCOLAT

TUFFY

VYLETTE

Lightning Source UK Ltd.
Milton Keynes UK
UKHW020914180223
417135UK00003B/225